P9-AFZ-203

Frog and Friends

Frog's Flying Adventure

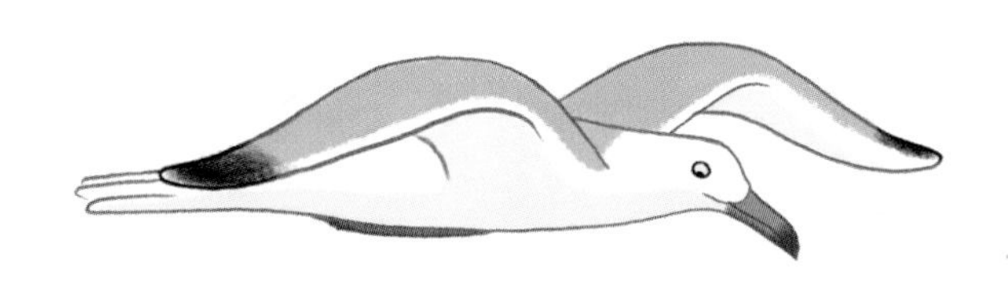

Written by Eve Bunting
Illustrated by Josée Masse

Again, for Keelin

—*Eve*

For my brother Christian.

—*Josée*

Sleeping Bear Press™
315 E. Eisenhower Parkway, Ste. 200
Ann Arbor, MI 48108
www.sleepingbearpress.com

Printed and bound in the United States.

10 9 8 7 6 5 4 3 2

Library of Congress Cataloging-in-Publication Data • Bunting, Eve, 1928- • Frog and friends: Frog's flying adventure / written by Eve Bunting; • illustrated by Josée Masse. • v. cm. • Summary: Frog finds a flower and tries to keep it alive, flies on his seagull friend's back, and gets help from his friends when he has trouble falling asleep. • Contents: A flower for Frog – Frog flies – Sleepy-time Frog. • ISBN 978-1-58536-805-1 (hardback) – ISBN 978-1-58536-806-8 (paper back) • [1. Frogs–Fiction. 2. Animals–Fiction. 3. Friendship–Fiction. 4. Ponds–Fiction.] I. Title. II. Title: Frog's flying adventure. • PZ7.B91527Fsf 2012 • [E]–dc23 • 2012007695

Table of Contents

A Flower for Frog

Frog was sunning on his rock when he saw something red.

It was in the long grass.

What is that? Frog wondered.

He hopped over to check.

It was a pretty red flower growing close to his pond.

Just to look at it made Frog happy.

"Come and see Flower," he told his friends. "Isn't she pretty?"

"Oh yes." His friends liked her as much as he did.

“Her name is Flower,” he told them.

Chameleon sighed. “That is a pretty name. It is easy to say. My name is hard to say.”

“We like it,” Little Jumping Mouse told him.

“It may be French,” Frog said.

“How did Flower get here?” Raccoon asked.

They thought about it.

“Maybe a friend of Frog’s brought it and left it there for him,” Rabbit said. “I left a carrot at my friend’s house this morning.”

Squirrel scratched his ear. “Maybe a bird dropped a seed. And Flower grew.”

“Or maybe it was magic,” Frog said.

Frog took good care of Flower.

He gave her water every day. “I know you need water,” he told her. “Frogs do, too.”

The grass grew thick around her. Frog cleared it away.

“Now you can feel the sun,” he told her.

Every morning he told Flower good morning.

Every night he told her good night.

It was like having a new friend.

But then, something bad happened.

The leaves on Flower began to droop.

She was not bright red anymore.

Frog was so worried he could not eat. Flies and moths and no-see-ums flew across his pond and he did not try to catch them. He thought about Flower.

The next day her edges were brown.

She had lost most of her petals.

All his friends came to visit her.

"We should sing to her," little Jumping Mouse said. "Singing might make her well again."

They gathered around her and sang a get-well song.

But Flower just stood, bent and almost bare.

"I am so sad," Frog said. "What more can I do for her?"

"Nothing," Raccoon said. "She has had her joy time. Now her time is past."

The little possums began to cry.

Then Squirrel stooped down and said, "**Wait!** Flower has left something for you, Frog."

Frog wiped his eyes. “What is it?”

“It is a little Flower. It has just started to grow. Soon it will be as big as Flower was.”

They all peered down.

"Oh my gosh!" Frog said. "Thank you, Flower. I will take good care of your little one . . .

"I will give her water and lots of sun. I will speak to her morning and night."

He smiled at his friends.

"What is her name?" Chameleon asked. "I hope it is a nice name."

"It is Little Flower," Frog said. "And I love her already."

Frog Flies

Sometimes Seagull flew over Frog's pond.

When he did, he stopped to float and talk.

“It must be nice to be able to fly,” Frog said.

"Yes, I go where I want to go. I see the world," said Seagull.

"There are things I want to see," Frog said. "I want to see a cow. And a horse. I want to see lots of things. But they are far from my pond."

"I can take you," Seagull said. "Here. Get on my back."

"Really? It will be safe?" Frog asked.

"Absolutely. I have been flying for years. I have never had an accident."

“All right. This will be an adventure,”

Frog said.

Frog climbed on Seagull's back.

Raccoon saw them take off.

“Come back, Frog,” she yelled. “Frogs do not fly.”

Frog waved.

“This one does!” he shouted.

They were going up. And up.

Oh, this was not good at all.

Frog clung to Seagull's feathers.

"You are pulling my feathers. It hurts!" Seagull yelled.

"Be careful! You are going too fast!" Frog yelled back. "Look out for that tree. You are going to hit it! If you are my friend, put me down. I do not like this. I am going to be sick. I am sliding off."

Frog wrapped his long legs around Seagull.

He had never been so afraid.

They flew over fields.

"**Look down!**" Seagull shouted.

"There is a horse. Look! There is a cow."

"**Yes! Yes!**" Frog screamed.

He had closed his eyes tight.

He opened them a little and looked down.

A horse. A cow.

His stomach hurt.

“We will go back now,” Seagull said.

“Yes, yes,” Frog said. “Back.”

“There is your pond,” Seagull told him.

Frog took his first deep breath. “Thank goodness.”

His pond was the nicest thing he had ever seen.

Seagull skimmed down.

Frog slid off his back.

His legs shook.

He bent over and kissed the ground.

“Now you have seen a cow and a horse,” Seagull told him.

Frog nodded. “Thank you, Seagull. Thank you for the nice ride.”

“You are welcome.” Seagull flew away.

All Frog's friends were waiting.

"Thank goodness," little Jumping Mouse told him.

"We were worried." Possum came and kissed his cheek. "Did you see a lot of interesting things?"

“Oh yes.” Frog tried to remember.

Was the black animal a cow or a horse?

Was the brown one a horse or a cow?

It didn’t matter. He had seen them both.

He had been on a great flying adventure.

And now he was home safely.

Life was good.

Sleepy-Time Frog

Frog sat on his rock.

"Are you all right, Frog?" Possum asked.

"I could not sleep last night. Or the night before."

Raccoon looked worried. "Why?"

"I do not know," Frog said.

"We will have to do something," Squirrel told him.

They went away.

When his friends came back that night Rabbit brought a cup of tea.

"It is carrot tea," she told Frog. "It will help you sleep."

"Thank you," Frog said.

Possum brought a book.

It was called *Sleepy-Time Stories.*

"My little possums love these stories," she said. "If you read them at night, you will sleep. I promise."

"Thank you," Frog said.

"I brought a lullaby," little Jumping Mouse said.

"What is a lullaby?" Frog asked.

"It is a go-to-sleep song. It will make you fall asleep and dream pretty dreams. I dream of chocolate."

"Thank you," Frog said.

“I will rub your feet,” Chameleon said. “If that is okay.”

“Yes, thank you,” Frog said.

Possum leaned forward to watch.

“You have very pretty feet,” she told Frog.

“I have been told so,” Frog agreed.

"I brought a bowl of bumblebee stew," Squirrel said. "I made it myself. It may not make you sleep. Or dream pretty dreams. But you will not be hungry if you are awake."

"Good idea," Frog said. "It smells so good."

They sat together on the grass in the light of the moon and the stars.

Frog passed around the carrot tea.

Possum read softly. Softly she turned the pages.

Little Jumping Mouse sang a lullaby.

"Lovely, lovely," Frog whispered.

A little breeze came to listen, then drifted on.

It was so good to have good friends.

Frog looked around.

Possum was asleep.

Her little possums were asleep.

Raccoon was asleep.

Squirrel was asleep.

Rabbit was asleep.

Chameleon was asleep, dark green on the dark green grass.

Little Jumping Mouse was asleep. Her whiskers twitched. “She is dreaming of chocolate,” Frog thought.

Frog ate some of the delicious bumble-bee stew.

He yawned, a big wide yawn.

Then he went to sleep, too.